*Eternal beauty can belong*
*To she who knows the siren's song.*
*She must attend with all her might*
*To gather these and hold them tight:*

*An eye of Cyclops, dragon's gore,* ✔
*The sharpest tooth of manticore,* ✔
*A phoenix feather scarcely grown,* ✔
*Unicorn's velvet newly thrown,* ✔
*Forelock of centaur young and fair,* ✔
*One golden lock of mermaid's hair.*

# SEA TALE

## GAIL E. HALEY

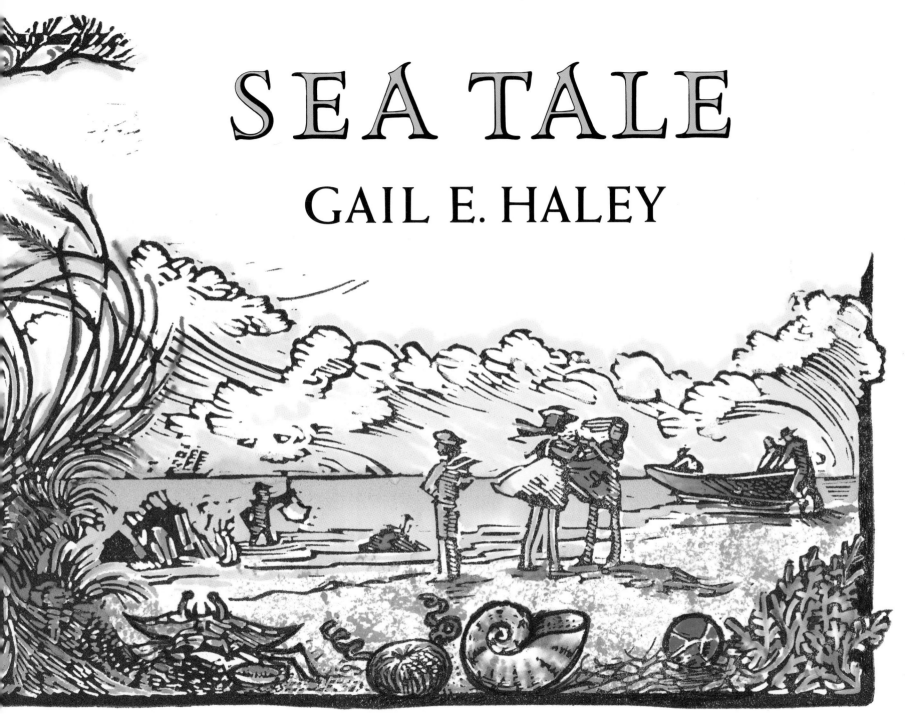

E. P. DUTTON   NEW YORK

Published in the United States by E. P. Dutton,
a division of Penguin Books USA Inc.
Published simultaneously in Canada by
Fitzhenry & Whiteside Limited, Toronto
Printed in Hong Kong by South China Printing Co.
First Edition    10 9 8 7 6 5 4 3 2 1

*Library of Congress Cataloging-in-Publication Data*
Haley, Gail E.
    Sea tale / by Gail E. Haley.      p.  cm.
    Summary: A young sailor's love for a mermaid is preserved in the
ring she fashions for him from a strand of her hair, but he finds
himself in a dire dilemma when he remembers he has promised a lock
of his sweetheart's hair to a mysterious old woman.
    ISBN 0-525-44567-6
    [1. Fairy tales.]   I. Title.           89-34453
PZ8.H135Se   1990                  CIP
[E]—dc20                            AC

for my husband, David

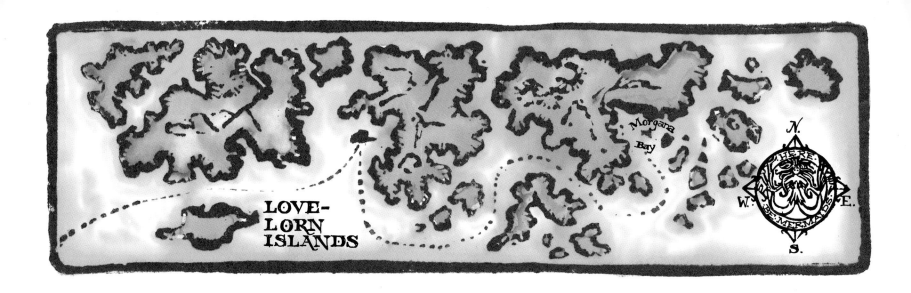

$T$om O'Shaunessy grew up by the sea. His toy boats were the vessels he would sail when he was a man. His sand castles were dreams of the real cities he would one day visit.

The sea brought him presents—coiled shells, bits of stone and glass worn into jewels, and mysterious pieces of sunken ships. But Tom's greatest treasures were his great-uncle Brian's tales. Captain Brian had explored the seven seas beyond the horizon.

Tom's favorite story was about the time Captain Brian sailed to the Lovelorn Islands. On a wee side trip, he discovered a secret place he called Morgana Bay. There he lost his heart to a sea maiden.

Though he had never returned to Morgana Bay, Brian had a map of the place tattooed on his chest. But Tom kept the map and story alive in his memory.

While still a lad, Tom was apprenticed to a master seaman. He took to sailing as if he'd been born for it. When he was grown, he commanded a great square-rigger, the *Stella Maris*, which he sailed to the four corners of the earth.

Through all his years at sea, he never lost a mate or damaged a cargo. But he had one failing for all of that. The shining stories of his childhood still filled his head. People laughed at his curious ideas and solitary ways.

Only old Gertie did not laugh. From her shop, The Siren's Song, down on the dock, she watched the comings and goings of seafaring men. She could tell their fortunes, tattoo pictures on their skin, and sell them charms for good luck.

She bought and traded for the peculiar things they brought back from their travels.

The day came when Tom, like others before him, happened by Gertie's shop.

"Have ye come to buy or trade?" Her eyes gleamed through the musty air.

"Well, Grannie, I've come for a golden mirror and comb. Something kind of dainty-like."

"I know what ye be searching for, lad, and I have the very thing." She pulled a dusty old box off of the very top shelf. From it she took a golden mirror and an ivory comb with a golden back.

"Aye," he murmured, "they are just as I dreamed they'd be. What's the price for these baubles?"

"I'll let ye have them for two shillings and a lock of your sweetheart's hair."

"But I don't have a sweetheart," Tom protested.

"Ah, but soon ye will. So you must swear an oath to bring me what I ask for."

Tom was only too eager for the trinkets. "How shall I swear?" he asked.

"You must swear . . .

By galleons tossed
and sailors lost—
I'll be true to my crew
and my oath to you.
And when I next set foot on this land,
I'll bring the thing you ask to you."

As Tom swore the oath, he could hear thunder in the distance. But outside, the sea and the sky were calm and blue.

The next day the *Stella Maris* set sail for the Lovelorn Islands. Tom knew he could trade for fine carvings and cloth to bring back, but it was his secret dream that really drew him there.

After weeks of sailing, they reached the largest of the Lovelorn Islands. Tom quickly struck his bargains with the king of the islands and had his crew exchange the goods. Then he dismissed them for three days of shore leave.

He gave care of the ship to his first mate, lowered the dinghy over the side, and set out in the moonlight. Tom pulled the oars with all his might, heading for the place Captain Brian had told him about. By morning he reached Morgana Bay. Ringed by coral reefs, it was just as he had seen it in his mind.

Tom anchored his dinghy and looked around. Not a mermaid was to be seen.

But his dream was stronger than his doubts. He tied a strong piece of twine around his wrist. He tied the other end round the handle of the mirror and lowered it into the clear water.

Little waves sprang up and washed against the dinghy. *Falilah, falilah* was the sound they made.

The boat rocked gently. The sun shone. Tom was tired from his hard night's work, and he dropped into a deep sleep.

Tom was awakened by a tugging on the string. Using all his strength, he pulled in his catch. Clinging to the mirror with both hands was a mermaid.

"Please don't take the moon eye away," she pleaded. "I've looked for one of these all my life."

"Ah, lass, it's a dear present you ask of me. If you want it, you must come into my boat and sing me a song."

So the mermaid flipped herself into Tom's dinghy. She was as beautiful as Tom had imagined, and her sweet song touched the very core of his heart.

"What is your name, Fish Maiden?" he stammered.

"I am Princess Falilah," she answered.

"What of the mirror, little Sea Princess? How did you know of such a toy?" Tom asked her.

"My grandmother had one like this when I was small. It was given to her by a land man. But he sailed away and never returned. She used to sit on the rocks and cry. One day she went to find him, and we never saw her again."

Falilah sat opposite Tom, combing her hair and looking into her new golden mirror. Tom sang songs to her that told of his feelings.

By the end of the day, they were hopelessly in love. Such things happen quickly in the Lovelorn Islands.

Falilah cut off a strand of her golden hair and wove it into a fine golden ring tied in a true lovers' knot.

"This ring contains the heart of Falilah," she said. "It will keep you safe on any sea. As long as you wear it, you can find your way back to me. If you lose it, you lose our love."

And to prove it was true, she called him down into the water.

Few men have seen the wonders Falilah showed Tom that night. Lantern fish and starfish and a hundred kinds of glowing plants lit up the seabed, so that it was as bright as any fairground.

Falilah called her court musicians: fiddler crabs, harpsichord anemones, great booming bass fish. And she taught Tom to dance an ocean minuet.

The night sped by as quickly as the day before.

In the morning they returned to the dinghy. Tom looked sadly at Falilah. "I'm bound to return to the ship, my love, for it is my duty to get my men safely home again."

"Don't leave me, Tom," pleaded the mermaid. "If you do, I may never see you again."

"I will come back to you, my love," said Tom. "On that you have my word. And my word is my honor." Tom kissed his fair love good-bye and set off in his dinghy.

Falilah was left weeping on the rocks, as her grandmother had been long ago.

Tom's crew was relieved to see him, and they set sail as soon as he came aboard the *Stella Maris*. All the long voyage home, Tom seemed changed. He kept mostly to the ship's helm, silent and alone.

At night he paced the deck or leaned over the stern of the ship. The waves that washed against its side whispered *Falilah*. His ears strained to hear her songs.

Out in the darkness something golden gleamed—as golden as the ring on his finger, as golden as mermaid hair.

When he slept, he dreamed of his sweetheart and her enchanted kingdom.

At last his home port was in sight. Through his spyglass he saw Gertie on the dock, rubbing her hands as she waited for her prize.

Tom's heart sank. Until this moment he had forgotten his oath to bring back a lock of his sweetheart's hair—the golden ring he wore on his finger.

If he gave Falilah's hair to Gertie, he would lose his sweetheart forever. Without Falilah's love and the promise of returning to her, Tom knew he could never be happy on land or sea.

Slowly he took to the dinghy and rowed till he was within earshot of Gertie.

"Give me what is mine!" she shouted.

"I've been true to my crew," crowed Tom, "and not untrue to you. I will never again set foot on land."

Without another word or a look back, Tom slipped over the side of his boat.

Nevermore did the sailor Tom O'Shaunessy set foot on the land of mortal man. But beneath the waves, there was a mermaid and the Tom she loved swimming back to the Lovelorn Islands.

Little waves whispered against the side of the *Stella Maris*:

*Falilah, Falilah, Falilah.*